For Fern and Sofia—R.W.

For Matt and my family,
all my love and thanks—H.S.

First U.S. edition 2002

Library of Congress Cataloging-in-Publication Data is available.

Library of Congress Catalog Card Number 2001058430

ISBN 0-7636-1953-1

First published in Great Britain in 2002 under the title
Wanted! Have You Seen This Alligator? by Gullane Children's Books Ltd.,
Stoneham Gate, Stoneham Lane, Eastleigh, Hampshire SO50 9NW

2 4 6 8 10 9 7 5 3 1

Printed in Belgium

This book was typeset in Bernhard Modern.
The illustrations were done in watercolor and colored pencil.

Candlewick Press
2067 Massachusetts Avenue
Cambridge, Massachusetts 02140

visit us at www.candlewick.com

Alberto
the Dancing Alligator

by
Richard Waring

illustrated by
Holly Swain

CANDLEWICK PRESS
CAMBRIDGE, MASSACHUSETTS

Tina was given a rather
large and peculiar-looking
egg by her Uncle Ezra.
She wrapped it in a soft
blanket and put it on
her bedside table.

That night, Tina heard a strange tapping
sound coming from the egg.
The shell began to crack, and a little snout
pushed its way out. Then two eyes appeared
and stared at her!
Tina gasped.

It was a baby
alligator!

Tina called the alligator
Alberto—Alberto Alligator.
She loved Alberto, and
Alberto loved her.
Very soon he grew into
a big alligator, and so Tina
kept him in the bathtub.

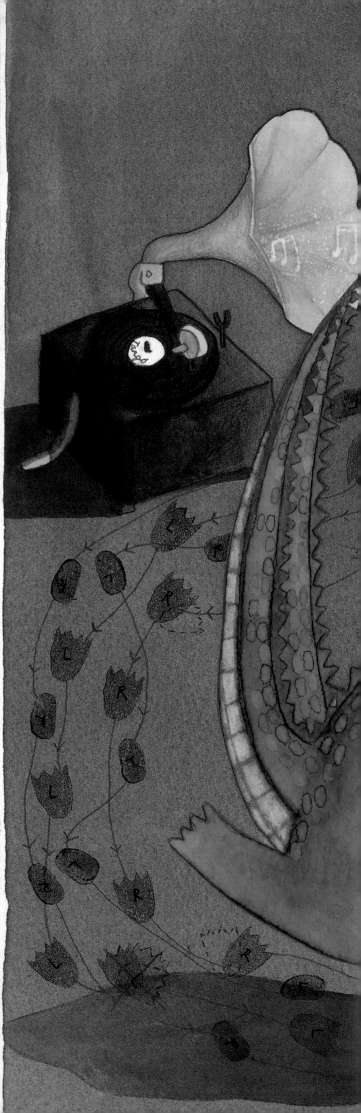

He loved music, particularly the tango, and they would dance together for hours to the sound of his favorite record . . .

. . . although he could never get the footing quite right.

Then, one day, a terrible thing happened.
While dancing in the bathroom, Tina and
Alberto **slipped** on a bar of soap.

Alberto fell headfirst into the toilet!
As Tina fell, she grabbed the toilet flusher,
and **WHOOSH** . . . .

. . . Alberto was **gone!**

Down, down, down went Alberto,
to the world way below the city.
Alberto thought it was
a great adventure.

He slid along pipes . . . . .

. . . . and splashed in large pools.

He played and swam . . .

. . . and swam and played.

Then, when he was tired, he decided it was time to go home.

Alberto climbed up one of the tall pipes until he reached a bathroom. But it was the wrong one! An old lady saw him, **screamed,** and called the police.

So Alberto climbed up the pipe that led to the next apartment. The plumber saw him,

screamed,

and also called the police.

...green...
...about 25 teeth...

Alberto went from bathroom to bathroom . . .

. . . and each time someone saw him, they screamed an

alled the police. That day, dozens of different people . . .

. . . called dozens of different police officers
to report an alligator in their bathroom.

The story was whispered around the police station. The police officers went home and told their neighbors about the alligators.

Very quickly, the rumor spread.
The newspaper reported:

1,000 ALLIGATORS ON THE LOOSE, ALL BATHROOMS AT RISK!

The mayor called the president, and the president

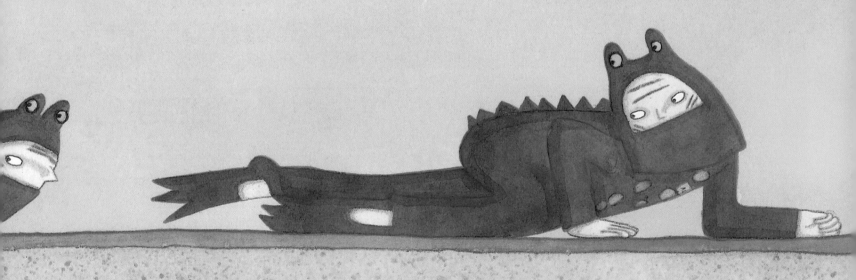

called the army, and the army called the experts.

Expert alligator hunters
went down into the deep,
dark, murky tunnels of the city's sewers.

The whole city was at a standstill. Everyone waited for the first alligator to be caught. Television and radio gave a moment-by-moment account of the search party's progress.

Tina and her dad saw the news.
They were both very worried for Alberto.
Tina ran to the bathroom and tried
calling Alberto's name loudly
down the toilet, but to no avail.

Then Tina had a better idea. . . .

Down in the sewers, Alberto could
hear the *splish*, *splash*, *swish*
of the alligator hunters.
He could see their shadows.
He was scared.
The hunters were getting closer
and closer to their target—
not one thousand alligators,
not even one hundred alligators . . .

. . . but one small, friendly but frightened Alberto.

Suddenly, a strange sound echoed through the tunnels . . .

. . . it was the music of the tango!
If an alligator could smile, he did.
It was Tina! She was playing his favorite record.

Alberto followed the sound as fast as he could.

...toward the music.

up

up

up

Up he climbed...

Alberto climbed
back into his
own bathroom.
Back to Tina.
He was safe at last.

Alberto hugged
Tina, and Tina
hugged Alberto.

When the search party
found nothing,
they gave up, and
the city soon forgot
all about alligators.

Alberto!

Tina took Alberto
to the animal sanctuary where
he now lives with the other alligators.
But he comes home every weekend . . .

. . . so they can practice their tango steps together.